PAPERBACK **PLUS**

P9-BYR-295

Contents

Cruz Martel

Cruz Martel is the pen name of a husband and wife writing team, Brent and Magalis Filson. Brent was born in Cleveland, Ohio. Magalis was born in a Puerto Rican village, Corral Viejo, and came to this country when she was seven years old.

Cruz Martel was Magalis's grandfather. "I have very fond memories of Cruz Martel," Magalis says. "He was a fisherman, very gruff, with sunburned, leathery skin. He was missing a few fingers on both his hands because of fishing accidents. But with me he was very gentle, very loving. I spent many wonderful hours curled up in his lap listening to stories he told in a deep, gravelly voice."

Ed Martinez

Ed Martinez was born in Buenos Aires, Argentina. He came to the United States as a young boy and studied art at Parsons School of Design, Pratt Institute, and the School of Visual Arts in New York City. He paints in oils, which give him the freedom to paint in bold brush-strokes. He likes to use local people he knows as models for his paintings.

Ed Martinez and his wife, Debbi Chabrian, are both artists. They live in an eighteenth-century house with separate studios. Martinez says, "We both work all the time, except when we're procrasti-nating!" Their young son, Oliver, is the newest addition to the family.

Yagua Days

written by Cruz Martel
pictures by Ed Martinez

HOUGHTON MIFFLIN COMPANY
BOSTON
ATLANTA DALLAS GENEVA, ILLINOIS PALO ALTO PRINCETON

Acknowledgments

For each of the selections listed below, grateful acknowledgment is made for permission to excerpt and/or reprint original or copyrighted materials, as follows:

Selections

"Mild and Sunny: The Climate of Puerto Rico," from *The World Book Encyclopedia*, Volume 15. Copyright © 1995 by World Book, Inc. Reprinted by permission.

"Rain Gauge," from *Simple Weather Experiments with Everyday Materials*, by Muriel Mandell. Copyright © 1991 by Muriel Mandell. Reprinted by permission of Sterling Publishing Co., Inc., 387 Park Ave. S., N.Y., 10016.

"The Water Cycle," from *Nature Detective: Weather*, by Anita Ganeri, illustrated by Mike Atkinson and Mark Machin. Copyright © 1993 by Franklin Watts. Reprinted by permission.

Yagua Days, by Cruz Martel. Text copyright © 1976 by Cruz Martel. Reprinted by permission of the author.

Photography

ii Courtesy of Cruz Martel. **iii** Courtesy of Ed Martinez. **41–43** Mark Bacon. **44** Tom Bean /DRK Photo. **45** Tim Holt/Photo Researchers (tl). **45** Tom Bean/Tony Stone Images (r). **45** Porterfield Chickering/Photo Researchers (bl). **46** Jeff Greenberg/Photo Researchers (t). **46–47** Suzanne Murphy/DDB Stock Photo. **47** Tony Arruza (bl). **48-49** Mark Bacon. **50-5I** Letraset.

2001 Impression

Houghton Mifflin Edition, 1996

Copyright © 1996 by Houghton Mifflin Company. All rights reserved.

No part of this work may be reproduced or transmitted in any form or by any means, electronic or mechanical, including photocopying and recording, or by any information storage or retrieval system without the prior written permission of the copyright owner unless such copying is expressly permitted by federal copyright law. With the exception of nonprofit transcription in Braille, Houghton Mifflin is not authorized to grant permission for further uses of this work. Permission must be obtained from the individual copyright owner as identified herein. Address requests for permission to make copies of Houghton Mifflin material to School Permissions, Houghton Mifflin Company, 222 Berkeley Street, Boston, MA 02116.

Printed in the U.S.A.

ISBN: 0-395-73235-2

I3 I4-B-02 0I 00

Yagua Days

It was drizzling steadily on the Lower East Side. From the doorway of his parents' *bodega*, Adán Riera watched a car splash the sidewalk.

School had ended for the summer two days ago, and for two days it had rained. Adán wanted to play in East River Park, but with so much rain about the only thing a boy could do was watch cars splash by.

Of course he could help his father. Adán enjoyed working in the *bodega*.
He liked the smells of the fruits and the different colors of the vegetables, and
he liked the way the *mangós*, *ñames*, and *quenepas* felt in his hands.

But today he would rather be in the park. He watched another car
spray past. The rain began to fall harder.

Mailman Jorge sloshed in, slapping water off his hat. He smiled.
"*¿Qué pasa*, Adán? Why the long face?"
"Rainy days are terrible days."
"No — they're wonderful days. They're *yagua* days!"

"Stop teasing, Jorge. Yesterday you told me the vegetables and fruits in the *bodega* are grown in panel trucks. What's a *yagua* day?"

"*Muchacho, this* day is a *yagua* day. And Puerto Rican vegetables and fruits *are* grown in trucks. Why, I have a truck myself. Every day I water it!"

Adán's mother and father came in from the back.

"*Hola*, Jorge. You look wet."

"I *feel* wetter. But it's a wonderful feeling. It's a *yagua*-day feeling!"

His mother and father liked Jorge. They had all grown up together in Puerto Rico.

"So you've been telling Adán about *yagua* days?"

"*Sí. Mira!* Here's a letter for you from Corral Viejo, where we all had some of the best *yagua* days."

Adán's father read the letter. "Good news! My brother Ulise wants Mami, Adán, and me to visit him on his *finca* for two weeks."

"You haven't been to Puerto Rico in years," said Mailman Jorge.

"Adán's *never* been there," replied his mother. "We can ask my brother to take care of the *bodega*. Adán will meet his family in the mountains at last."

Adán clapped his hands. "Puerto Rico! Who cares about the rain!"

Mailman Jorge smiled. "Maybe you'll even have a few *yagua* days. *Hasta luego. Y que gocen mucho!*"

Tío Ulise met them at the airport in Ponce.

"Welcome to Puerto Rico, Adán."

Stocky Uncle Ulise had tiny blue eyes in a round, red face, and big, strong arms, but Adán, excited after his first plane ride, hugged Uncle Ulise even harder than Uncle Ulise hugged him.

"Come, we'll drive to Corral Viejo." He winked at Adán's father. "I'm sorry you didn't arrive yesterday. Yesterday was a wonderful *yagua* day."

"You know about *yagua* days too, tío Ulise?"

"Sure. They're my favorite days."

"But wouldn't today be a good *yagua* day?"

"The worst. The sun's out!"

In an old jeep, they wound up into the mountains.
"Look!" said Uncle Ulise, pointing at a river jumping rocks.

"Your mother and father, Mailman Jorge, and I played in that river
when we were children."

They bounced up a hill to a cluster of bright houses. Many people were outside.

"This is your family, Adán," said Uncle Ulise.

Everyone crowded around the jeep. Old and young people.
Blond-, brown-, and black-haired people. Dark-skinned and light-skinned

people. Blue-eyed, brown-eyed, and green-eyed people. Adán had not
known there were so many people in his family.

Uncle Ulise's wife Carmen hugged Adán and kissed both his
cheeks. Taller than Uncle Ulise and very thin, she carried herself like a
soldier. Her straight mouth never smiled — but her eyes did.

The whole family sat under wide trees and ate *arroz con gandules*, *pernil*, *viandas* and *tostones*, *ensaladas de chayotes y tomates*, and *pasteles*.

Adán talked and sang until his voice turned to a squeak.

He ate until his stomach almost popped a pants button.

Afterward he fell asleep under a big mosquito net before the sun had even gone down behind the mountains.

In the morning Uncle Ulise called out, "Adán, everyone ate all the food in the house. Let's get more."

"From a *bodega?*"

"No, *mi amor*. From my *finca* on the mountain."

"You drive a tractor and plow on the mountain?"

Tía Carmen smiled with her eyes. "We don't need tractors and plows on our *finca*."

"I don't understand."

"*Vente*. You will."

Adán and his parents, Aunt Carmen, and Uncle Ulise hiked up the mountain beside a splashy stream.

Near the top they walked through groves of fruit trees.

"Long ago your grandfather planted these trees," Adán's mother said. "Now Aunt Carmen and Uncle Ulise pick what they need for themselves or want to give away or sell in Ponce."

"Let's work!" said Aunt Carmen.

Sitting on his father's shoulders, Adán picked oranges.

Swinging a hooked stick, he pulled down *mangós*.

Whipping a bamboo pole with a knife tied to the end, he chopped *mapenes* from a tall tree.

Digging with a machete, he uncovered *ñames*.

Finally, gripping a very long pole, he struck down coconuts.

"How do we get all the food down the mountain?" he asked.

"Watch," said Aunt Carmen. She whistled loudly.

Adán saw a patch of white moving in the trees. A horse with a golden mane appeared.

Uncle Ulise fed him a *guanábana*. The horse twitched his ears and munched the delicious fruit loudly.

"Palomo will help us carry all the fruit and vegetables we've picked," Adán's mother said.

Back at the house, Adán gave Palomo another *guanábana*.

"He'll go back up to the *finca* now," his father said. "He's got all he wants to eat there."

Uncle Ulise rubbed his knee.

"*¿Qué te pasa?*" asked Adán's mother.

"My knee. It always hurts just before rain comes."

Adán looked at the cloudless sky. "But it's not going to rain."

"Yes, it will. My knee never lies. It'll rain tonight. Maybe tomorrow. Say! When it does, it'll be a *yagua* day!"

In the morning Adán, waking up cozy under his mosquito net, heard rain banging on the metal roof and *coquís* beeping like tiny car horns.

He jumped out of bed and got a big surprise. His mother and father, Uncle Ulise, and Aunt Carmen were on the porch wearing bathing suits.

"*Vámonos*, Adán," his father said. "It's a wonderful *yagua* day. Put on your bathing suit!"

In the forest he heard shouts and swishing noises in the rain.

Racing into a clearing, he saw boys and girls shooting down a runway of grass, then disappearing over a rock ledge.

Uncle Ulise picked up a canoelike object from the grass. "This is a *yagua*, Adán. It fell from this palm tree."

"And this is what we do with it," said his father. He ran, then belly-flopped on the *yagua*. He skimmed down the grass, sailed up into the air, and vanished over the ledge. His mother found another *yagua* and did the same.

"Papi! Mami!"

Uncle Ulise laughed. "Don't worry, Adán. They won't hurt themselves. The river is down there. It pools beneath the ledge. The rain turns the grass butter-slick so you can zip into the water. That's what makes it a *yagua* day! Come and join us!"

That day Adán found out what fun a *yagua* day is!

Two weeks later Adán lifted a box of *mangós* off the panel truck back in New York.

"*Hola, muchacho!* Welcome home!"

Adán smiled at Mailman Jorge. "You look sad, *compadre.*"

"Too much mail! Too much sun!"

"What you need is a *yagua* day."

"So you know what a *yagua* day is?"

"I had six *yagua* days in Puerto Rico."

"You went over the ledge?"

"Of course."

"Into the river?"

"*Sí! Sí!* Into the river. Sliding on *yaguas!*"

"Two-wheeled or four-wheeled *yaguas?*"

Adán laughed. "*Yaguas* don't have wheels. They come from palm trees."

"I thought they came from panel trucks like mine."

"Nothing grows in trucks, Jorge. These *mangós* and oranges come from trees. The *gandules* come from bushes. And the *ñames* come from under the ground. *Compadre*, wake up. Don't you know?"

Mailman Jorge laughed. "Come, *campesino*, let's talk with your parents. I want to hear all about your visit to Corral Viejo!"

Spanish Word List

arroz con gandules [ah-ROHZ kon ghan-DOO-les] - rice with
    pigeon peas

bodega [boh-DEG-ah] - Puerto Rican grocery store

buenos días [BWEN-noss DEE-ahs] - good day or hello

campesino [kham-peh-SEE-noh] - country boy

chayotes [chah-YOH-tahs] - a squash-like fruit

compadre [kom-PA-dreh] - pal

coquís [koh-KEES] - tree frogs

ensaladas de chayotes y tomates [en-sah-LAH-dahs deh chah-YOH-tehs
    ee toh-MAH-tehs] - salads of *chayotes* and tomatos

finca [FEEN-kah] - plantation

guanábana [ghwah-NAH-bah-nah] - a sweet, pulpy fruit, slightly smaller
    than a football, covered with prickly skin

hasta luego [AH-stah loo-WEH-goh] - till we meet again; good-bye

hola [OH-la] - hello

mami [MAH-mee] - mommy

mangó [mahn-GO] - a sweet, tropical fruit, golden when ripe

mapenes [mah-PEN-nehs] - breadfruit, also known as *panapenes*
    [pah-nah-PEN-nehs]

mi amor [mee ah-MOHR] - my love

mira [MEE-rah] - look

muchacho [moo-CHA-choh] - boy

ñame [NYAH-meh] - a tropical root vegetable similar to a potato

papi [PAH-pee] - daddy

pasteles [pahs-TELL-ehs] - Puerto Rican dumplings

pernil [pehr-NEEL] - roast pork

plátano [PLAH-ta-noh] - a tropical fruit similar to a banana

¿qué pasa? [keh PAH-sah] - What's happening?

¿qué te pasa? [keh teh PAH-sah] - What's the matter?

quenepa [keh-NEH-pah] - a grape-sized fruit with a hard, green peel

sí [see] - yes

tía [TEE-ah] - aunt

tío [TEE-oh] - uncle

tostones [tohs-TOH-nehs] - fried green plantains

vámonos [BAH-moh-nohs] - let's go

vente [BEN-teh] - come on

viandas [vee-AHN-dahs] - general term for Puerto Rican vegetables

y que gocen mucho [ee keh GOH-sen MOO-choh] - and have fun!

yagua [JAH-gwah] - the seed pod of the Puerto Rican royal palm tree

Sunny and Mild
The Climate of

by Fernando Bayrón-Toro

Puerto Rico's pleasant climate makes the island a popular vacation spot. The climate also provides good conditions for growing crops. Temperatures average about 73° F (23° C) in January and 80° F (27° C) in July. Frost and snow never occur, and even hail is rare. Sea breezes make the climate much more comfortable in summer than it is in the central United States.

In many parts of the island, some rain falls nearly every day. The rainfall is usually heavy, but it lasts only a short time. The drier sections of the southern coast average 37 inches (94 centimeters) of rain a year. Rainfall in the north averages 70 inches (180 centimeters) a year. A rain forest on El Yunque, a mountain, sometimes gets over 200 inches (510 centimeters) a year.

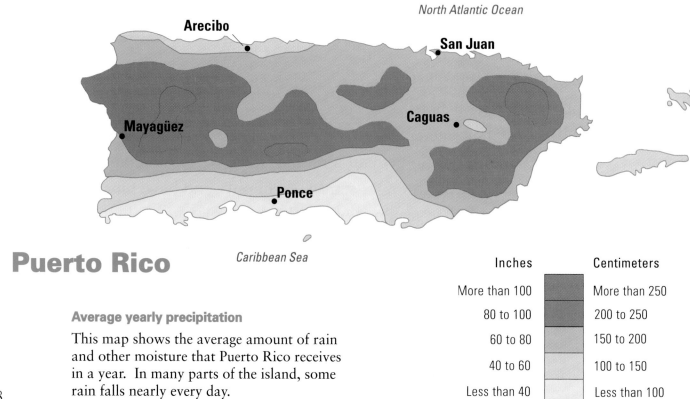

North Atlantic Ocean

Arecibo

San Juan

Caguas

Mayagüez

Ponce

Caribbean Sea

Puerto Rico

Average yearly precipitation

This map shows the average amount of rain and other moisture that Puerto Rico receives in a year. In many parts of the island, some rain falls nearly every day.

Inches		Centimeters
More than 100		More than 250
80 to 100		200 to 250
60 to 80		150 to 200
40 to 60		100 to 150
Less than 40		Less than 100

Puerto Rico

People in Puerto Rico must be alert for hurricanes from June through November. But severe hurricanes occur only once every 10 years, on the average. These storms are predicted hours or even days in advance by the National Weather Service. The storm warnings are announced by newspapers, radio, and television so that people have time to take shelter in strong buildings.

The highest temperature ever recorded in Puerto Rico, 103° F (39° C), occurred at San Lorenzo on August 22, 1906. The lowest temperature, 40° F (40° C), was recorded at Aibonito on March 9, 1911.

Average monthly weather

San Juan					
	Temperatures				Days of rain or snow
	F°		C°		
	High	Low	High	Low	
Jan.	80	70	27	21	20
Feb.	80	70	27	21	14
Mar.	81	71	27	22	14
Apr.	82	72	28	22	14
May	84	74	29	23	16
June	84	75	29	24	17
July	84	76	29	24	19
Aug.	85	76	29	24	20
Sept.	86	75	30	24	18
Oct.	85	75	29	24	18
Nov.	83	74	28	23	19
Dec.	81	72	27	22	20

Regions of hurricane activity
Hurricanes develop over warm ocean water. They weaken after moving over land areas. This map shows the regions in which most hurricanes occur.

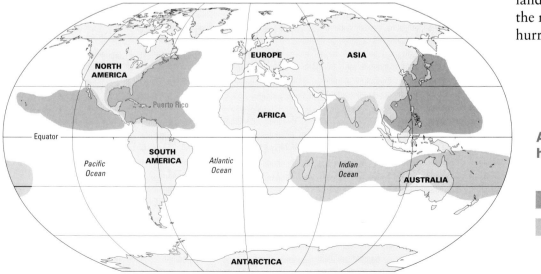

Average number of hurricanes per year

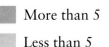

More than 5

Less than 5

The Water Cycle

by Anita Ganeri

Over two-thirds of the earth is covered in water. It lies in the oceans, lakes, and rivers, and is frozen in the ice caps. Water is also present in the atmosphere in its gas form, water vapor, and falls to earth as rain or snow. But any rain you see has already fallen billions of times before. This is because no new water is ever made on earth. The existing supply is recycled and reused time after time, in a continuous process called the water cycle.

In the water cycle, the sun heats the water in the oceans. It evaporates (turns into water vapor) and rises into the air. As it rises, it cools and condenses (turns into droplets of liquid water) into rain or condenses and then freezes into snow. This rain or snow falls back into the oceans or is carried by rivers to the sea. Billions of gallons of water evaporate from the oceans each day. The atmosphere contains enough water vapor to cover the earth with a layer three feet deep.

Isla del encanto
Island of Enchantment
A Puerto Rican Photo Album

PUERTO RICO is a tropical island located between the Atlantic Ocean and the Caribbean Sea. The island is about 100 miles long and 35 miles wide.

Over three million people live in Puerto Rico. The island is a commonwealth of the United States. That means that Puerto Ricans are citizens of the United States. However, unlike citizens who live in the United States, Puerto Ricans who live in Puerto Rico do not vote for President. Puerto Ricans elect their own governor. The Puerto Rican government works with the government of the United States.

Riding the *Yagua*

In some areas, Puerto Rican kids have fun riding on *yaguas*. *Yaguas* are the empty seed pods of the Puerto Rican royal palm tree. As the tree grows, the *yaguas* fall to the ground. Kids collect the *yaguas* and choose a good hill for sliding.

Sliding is especially good on rainy days when the grass is wet and slippery. Some kids also use the pavement for their yagua rides!

A Puerto Rican royal palm shows a *yagua* peeling off the tree.

Kids prepare the *yagua* for a ride.

A friendly push helps this boy get a good start.

The *yagua*-riders zoom down the hill!

Views of the Island

Puerto Rico is an island of cities, mountains, beaches, and tropical countryside. The El Yunque rain forest, located in the mountains of Puerto Rico, contains many types of colorful birds and flowers. It rains four times a day there!

Many visitors to Puerto Rico travel to the southern city of Ponce. There, they can see many sights, such as famous art galleries and beautiful plazas.

Rolling hills and valleys are typical of the countryside.

Royal palms lean over a sandy beach on the coast.

The Fountain of Lions adorns the main plaza of Ponce.

Lush tropical plants grow in the El Yunque rain forest.

All Kinds of People

Puerto Rico has had a long history of people settling on the island. Many Puerto Ricans can trace their roots back to Spain, other countries in Europe, Africa, Asia, and Latin America. Recently, more and more Puerto Ricans are living in the United States. For example, over one million Puerto Ricans live in New York City.

A man who sells fruits and vegetables talks with his customers.

Two friends pose for the camera.

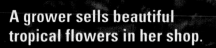
A grower sells beautiful tropical flowers in her shop.

Schoolchildren stay together on a class trip.

School girls join their friends after school.

47

Tasty Tropical Fruits

Granadilla pulp has the same taste as *granada*, or pomegranate.

The mix of sun and rain makes Puerto Rico a perfect place for growing fruits. The bananas, pineapples, and coconuts you eat may come from Puerto Rico. Other tropical fruits that grow in Puerto Rico are plantains, *mangós*, and star apples.

A *mangó* tree bears sweet fruit that turns golden as it gets ripe.

Mapenes, also called *panapenes*, or breadfruit, have a texture like bread when baked or roasted.

A *guanábana* is a sweet, pulpy fruit slightly smaller than a football.

Quenepa is a grape-sized fruit with a hard, green peel.

A *plátano*, or plantain, is similar to a banana.

A fruit stand displays colorful tropical fruits.

Experiment With Weather

by Muriel Mandell

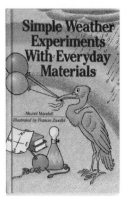

How Much Rain Is There Where You Live?

Make a Rain Gauge

Measure the amount of rain that falls during a period of a week or a month, and compare your results with the official statistics.

You need:

various containers (a coffee can, a jar, a cut down milk carton)
masking tape
a ruler

What to do:

Using a ruler, measure off inches or centimeters on strips of masking or adhesive tape. Attach the tapes to the various containers.

Put the containers in a flat, level open place. A windowsill will do fine. (It may be wise to place them in a box to make sure they remain upright.)

Each time it rains, measure the amount of rain in the containers. The levels should be the same whatever the size of the container, provided that its sides are parallel. Record the amount and date.

Compare measurements from one rainfall to the next. And compare your measurements with those announced on TV or radio. They may not always agree. Sometimes, the amount of rain varies from one side of the street to the other!